WARNING:
CHUNKS
WILL FLY!

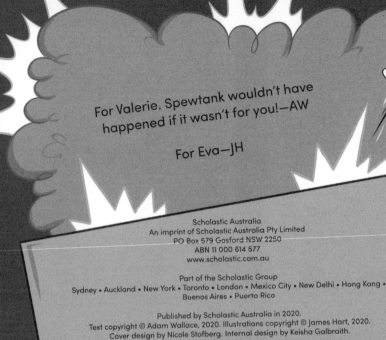

For Valerie. Spewtank wouldn't have happened if it wasn't for you!—AW

For Eva—JH

Scholastic Australia
An imprint of Scholastic Australia Pty Limited
PO Box 579 Gosford NSW 2250
ABN 11 000 614 577
www.scholastic.com.au

Part of the Scholastic Group
Sydney • Auckland • New York • Toronto • London • Mexico City • New Delhi • Hong Kong • Buenos Aires • Puerto Rico

Published by Scholastic Australia in 2020.
Text copyright © Adam Wallace, 2020. Illustrations copyright © James Hart, 2020.
Cover design by Nicole Stofberg. Internal design by Keisha Galbraith.

 A catalogue record for this book is available from the National Library of Australia

ISBN: 978-1-76097-242-4

Typeset in Bree.

Printed in China by Hang Tai Printing Company Limited.

Scholastic Australia's policy, in association with Hang Tai, is to use papers that are renewable and made efficiently from wood grown in responsibly managed forests, so as to minimise its environmental footprint.

10 9 8 7 6 5 4 3 2   22 23 24 25 / 2

FARTBOY
ENTER THE SPEWTANK

ADAM
WALLACE

JAMES HART

A Scholastic Australia Book

Previously on . . .

FARTBOY

Martin was just **an ordinary boy** who lived with his mum and dad.

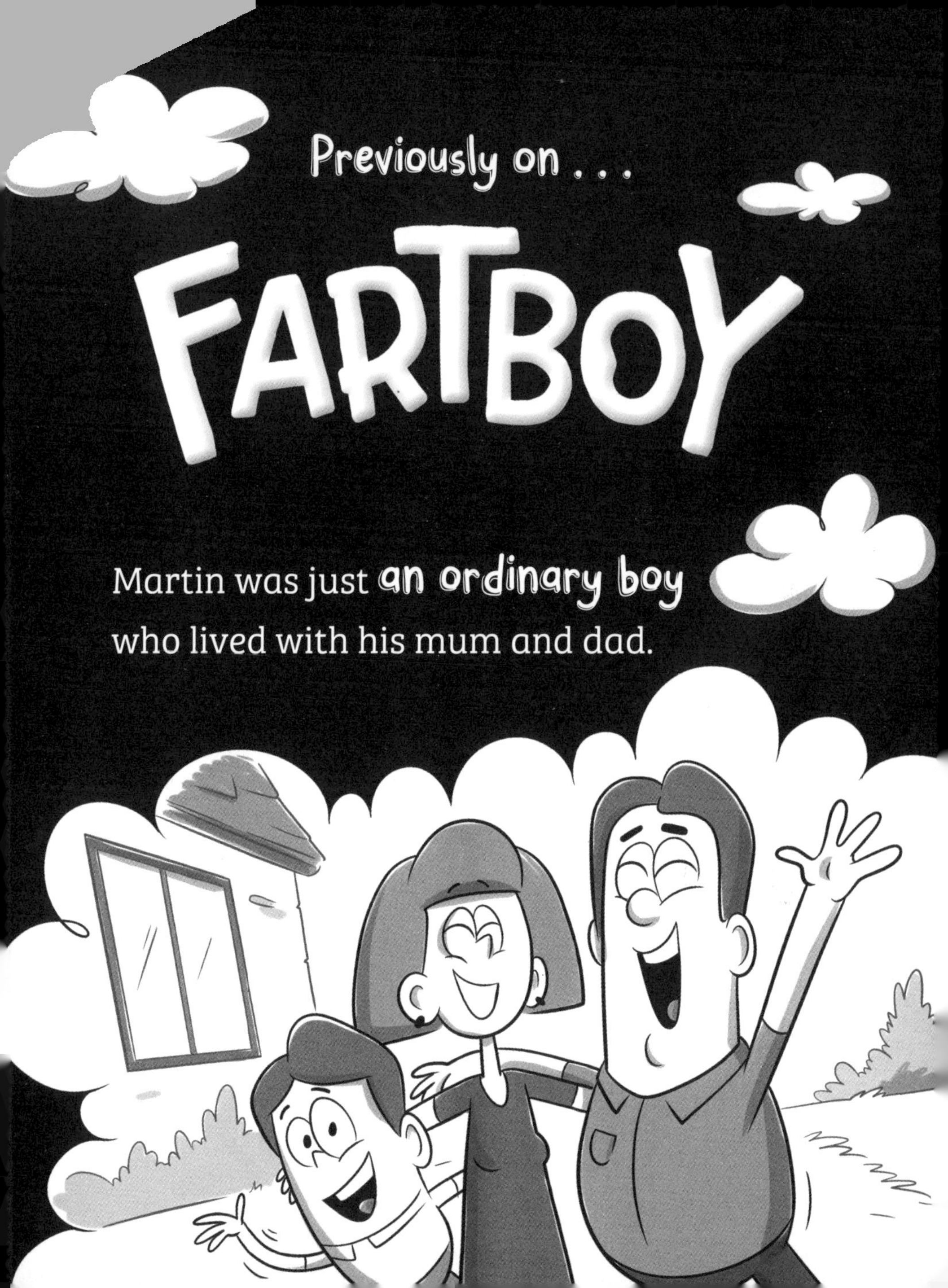

More than anything, he loved being **clean and tidy.** And he never, ever farted.

Then a freaky, *fart gas explosion* at **THE BAKED BEANS FACTORY** changed everything.

Martin **lost his parents** and his sense of smell . . .

. . . But gained a **long-lost grandma,**

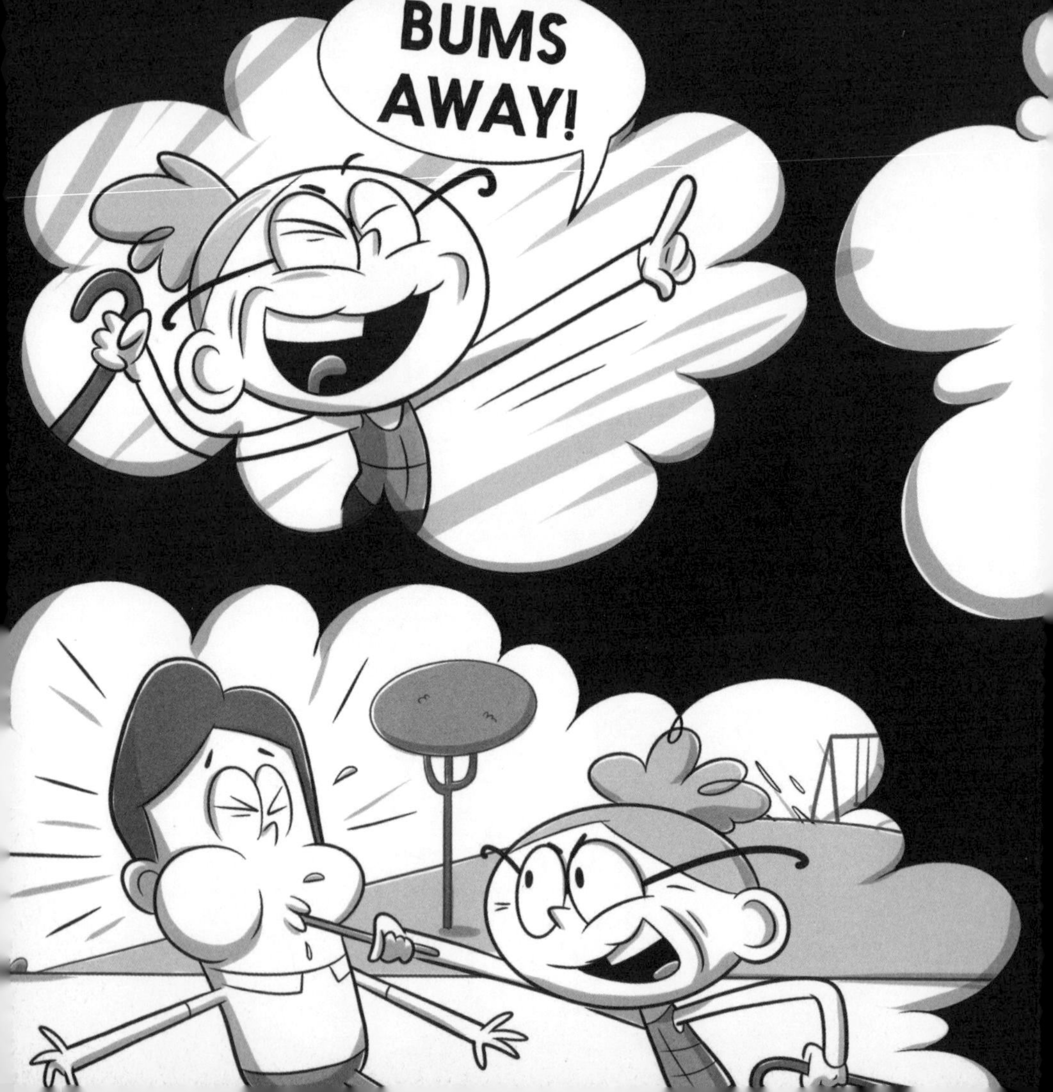
BUMS AWAY!

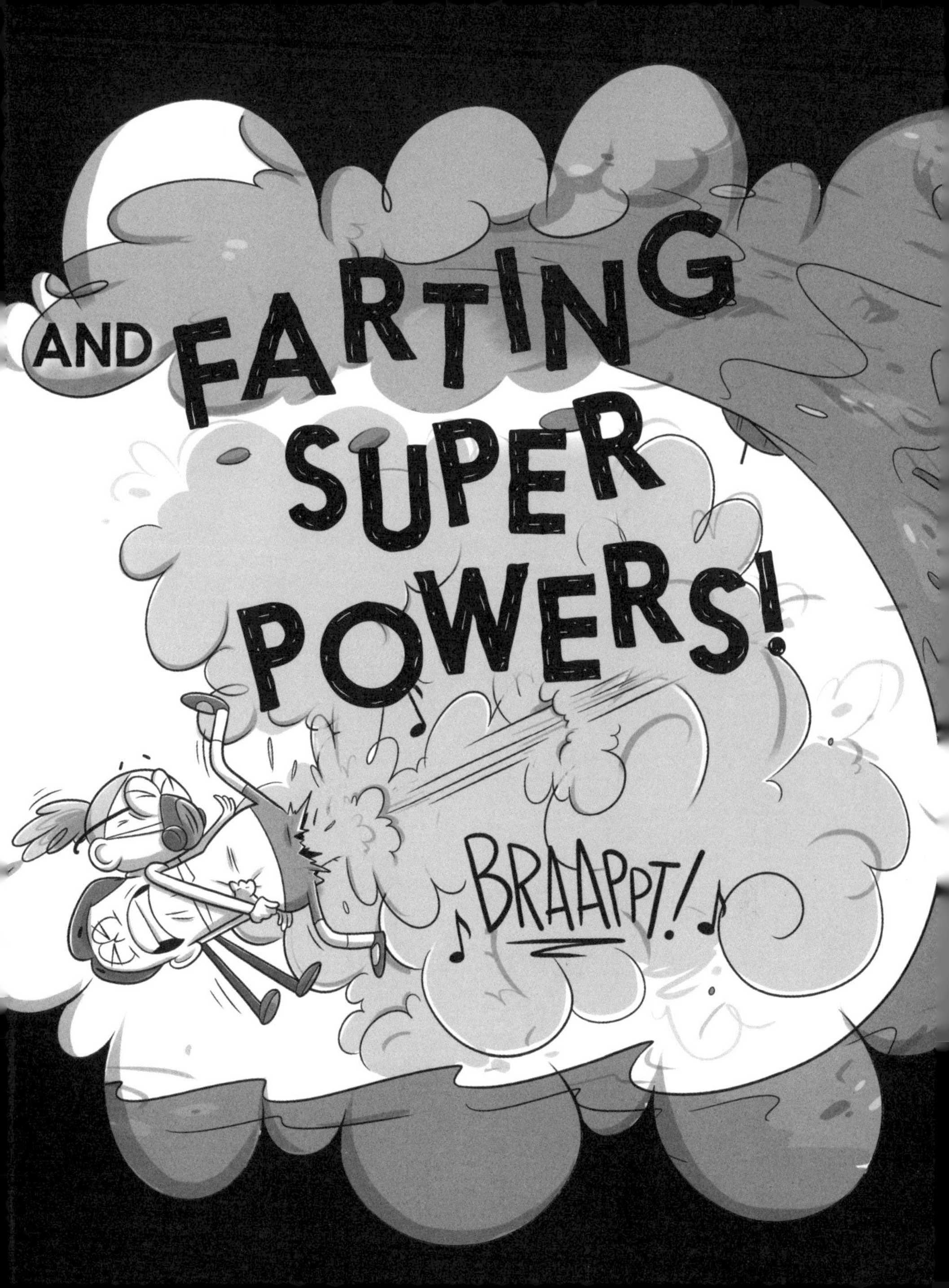
AND FARTING SUPER POWERS!
BRAAPPT!

Martin became **FARTBOY!**

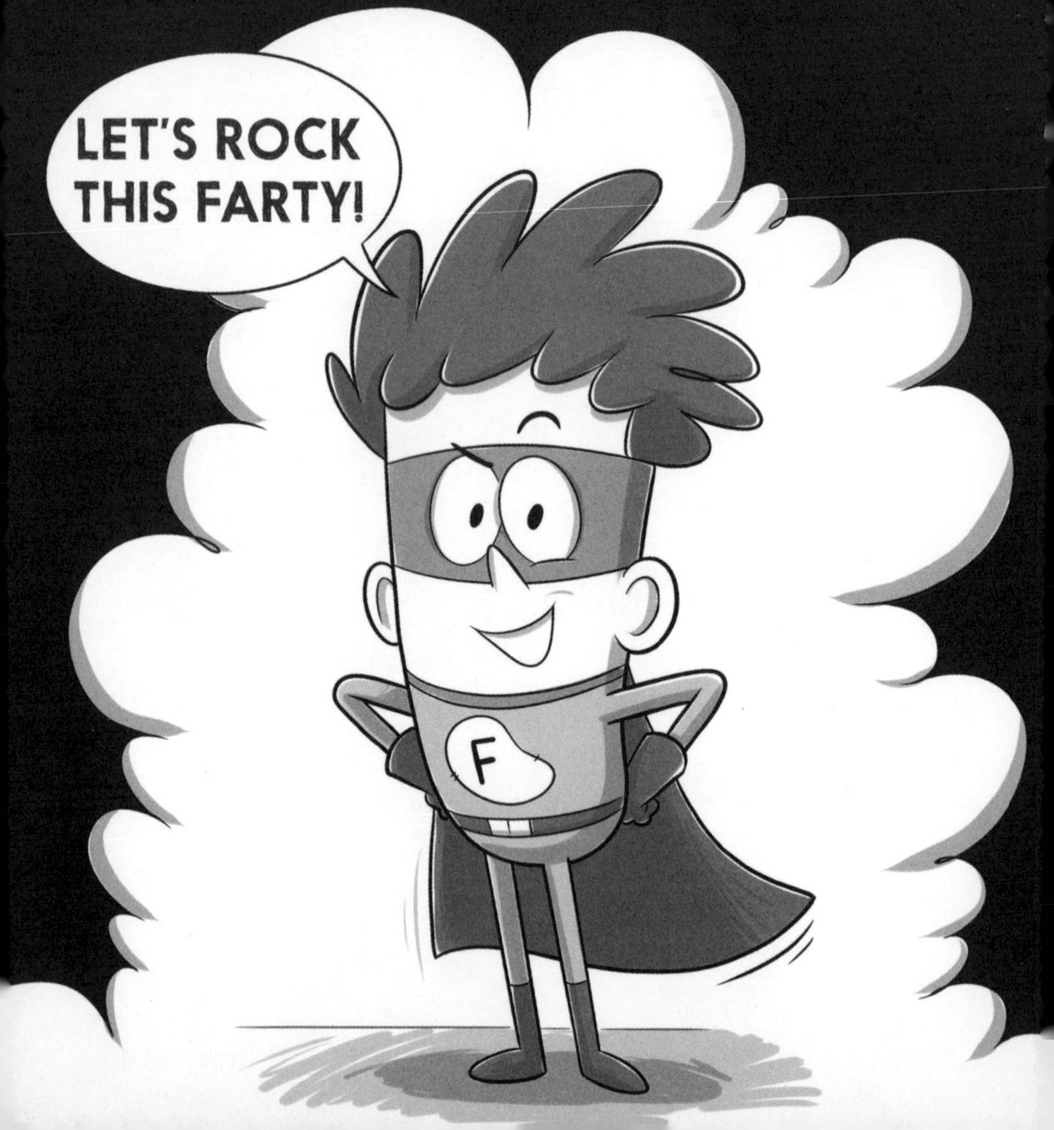
LET'S ROCK THIS FARTY!

NEWS FLASH!

In breaking news ... DON'T BREAK ANYTHING! Seriously! The **World's Tidiest Town Judging Committee** are coming to judge Sparkletown *TOMORROW!* Do you know what this means?

Our seventeen-year reign is at risk—so brush that floor, mop those teeth, wipe that carpet and, for heaven's sake, **vacuum that butt!**

In other news, a new villain is on the scene, and this villain is a lean, mean, spewing machine! **SPEWTANK** is the name, and graffiti is the game. Chunky, smelly graffiti.

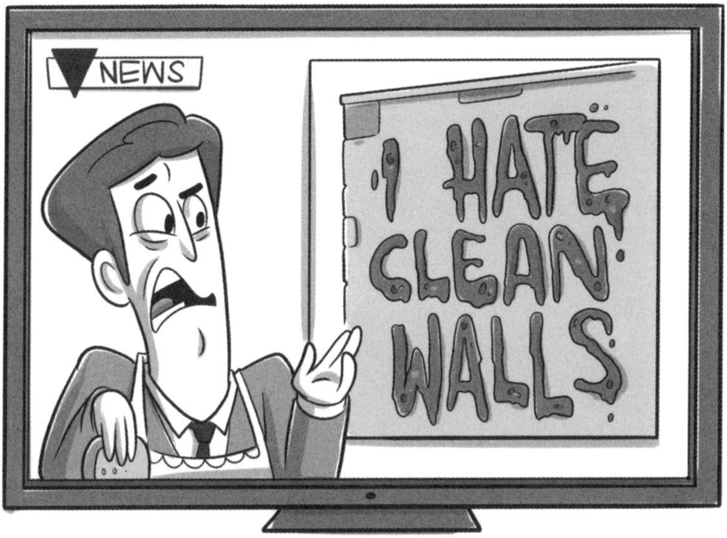
NEWS
I HATE CLEAN WALLS

Will **SPEWTANK** ruin everything this town holds dear? Fartboy, you stinky wonder, we need your amazing bottom to save the day!

We now return you to your regular programming, *Cows Say Moo.*

TOO BiG FOR MY BUTT

Grandma switched off the TV. 'We HAVE to stop **SPEWTANK** ruining the city, Martin.'

'It's no problem, Grandma, didn't you hear? **Stinky wonder? Amazing bottom?** *I'll* stop **SPEWTANK** and we'll win the **World's Tidiest Town** for the eighteenth year in a row and everyone will love Fartboy even more!'

But Grandma looked worried. 'Of course I know that. I just feel maybe you're getting **too big for your boots.**'

'Or too big for my *butts?*' I asked.

Who knew that I, Martin Kennedy, the **cleanest kid** in the world, would love being the grossest, most **disgusting superhero** ever?

I could say it now. '**I LOVE BEING A FARTER!**'

Grandma looked even more worried. 'Martin, I am proud and concerned at the same time. Now, get your butt into gear. **SPEWTANK** is on the rampage. So you need another lesson at FART SCHOOL!'

TO THE TRAINING ROOM!

Be clean with Beans

'Martin, go get all your fluffy toys,' said Grandma.

I blushed. 'I don't have fluffy toys.'

What about all the ones lined up in your cupboard where you think I can't see them?

Oh, those old things? Hahaha, they're from when I was a baby.

I saw you cleaning them last week.

They were dusty.

20

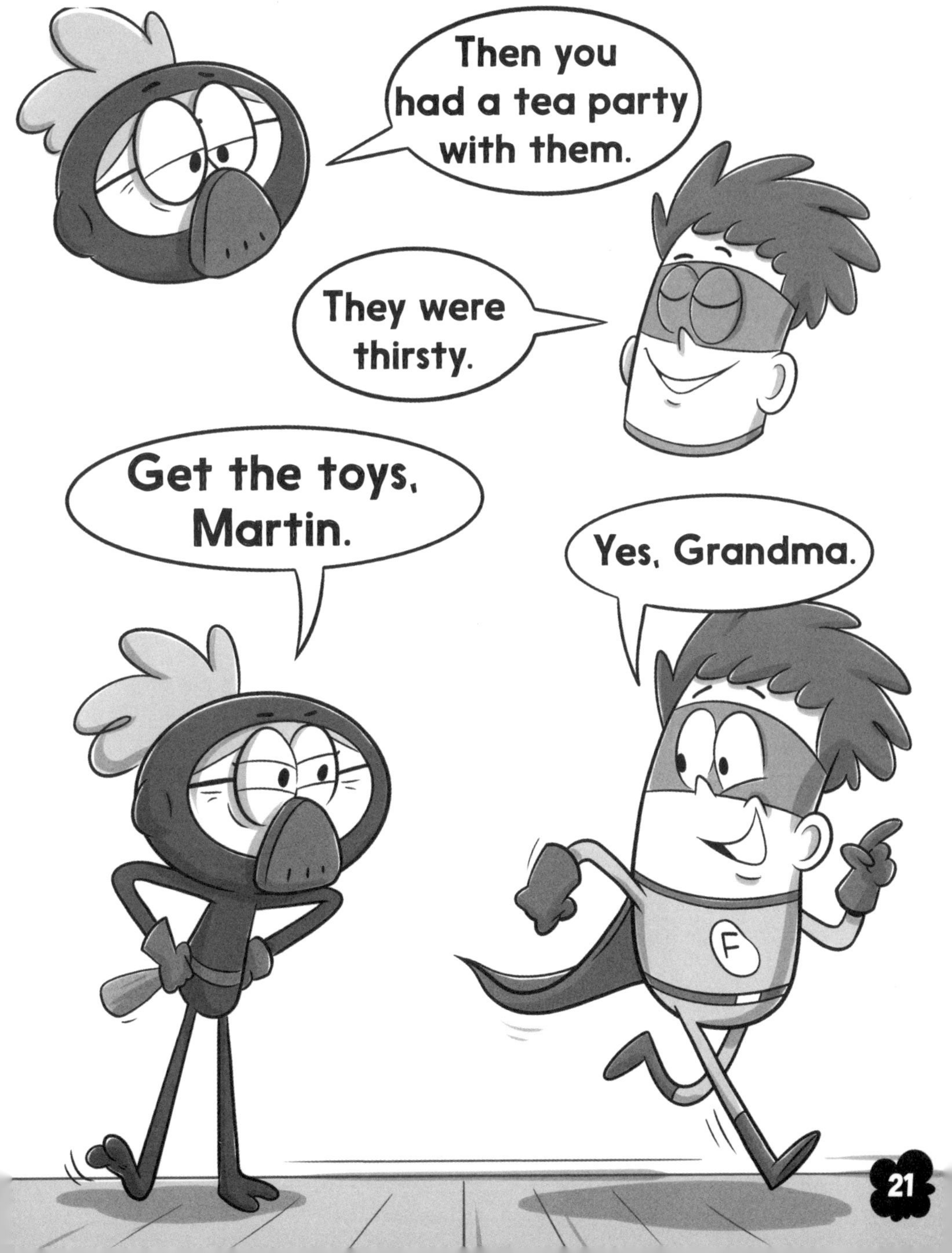
Then you had a tea party with them.
They were thirsty.
Get the toys, Martin.
Yes, Grandma.

'Now,' Grandma said. 'By controlling the power of your rear end, you can remove the dirt. I call this class: BEAN CLEAN 101!'

I was shocked.

My **BOTTY BOMBS** can *clean?*

'They will **blast the dirt away.** Try it!'

Grandma lined up the toys and put dirt all over **Mr Tinkles, Little Miss Moo Moo** and Minky Monkey.

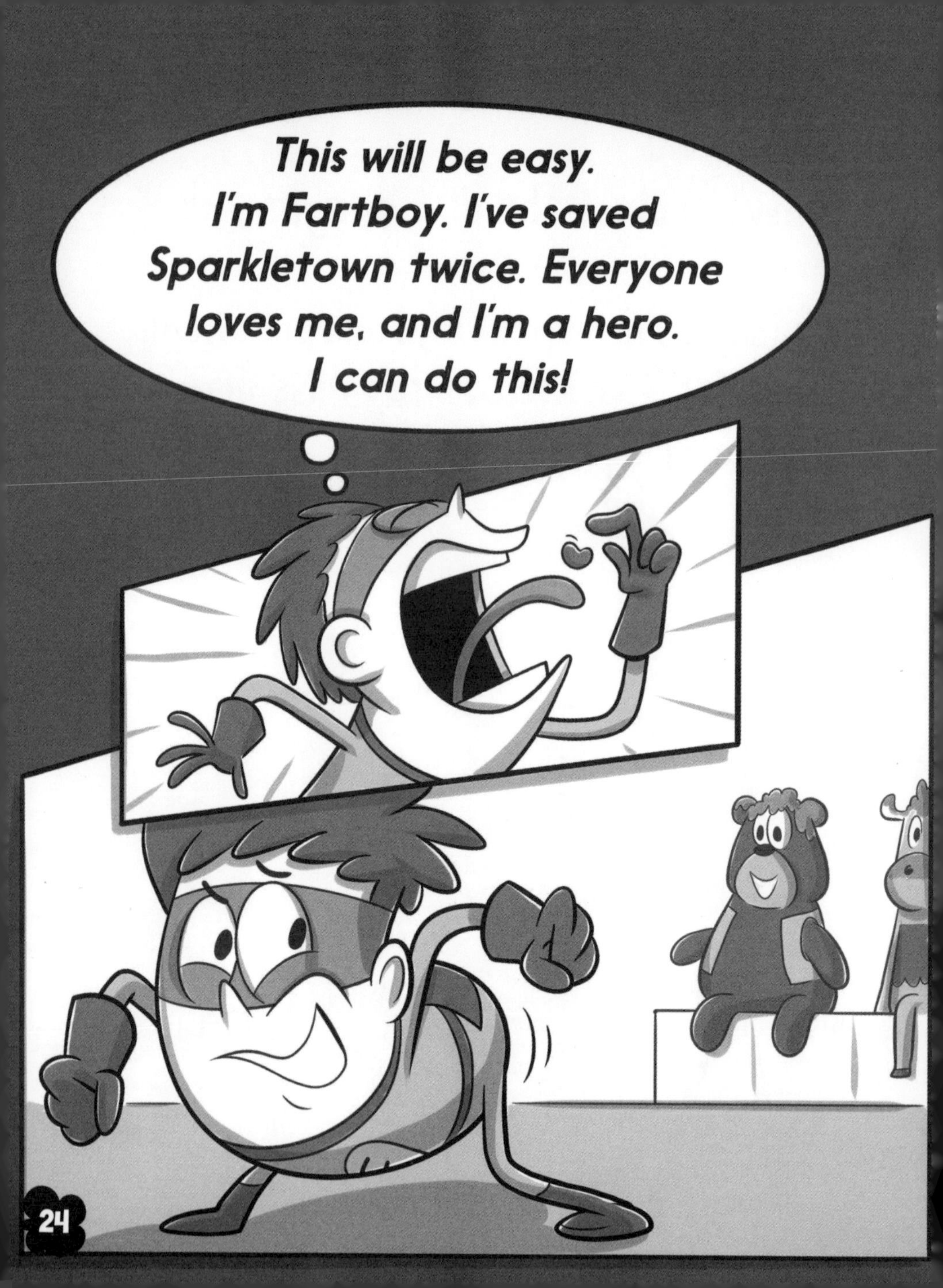
This will be easy. I'm Fartboy. I've saved Sparkletown twice. Everyone loves me, and I'm a hero. I can do this!

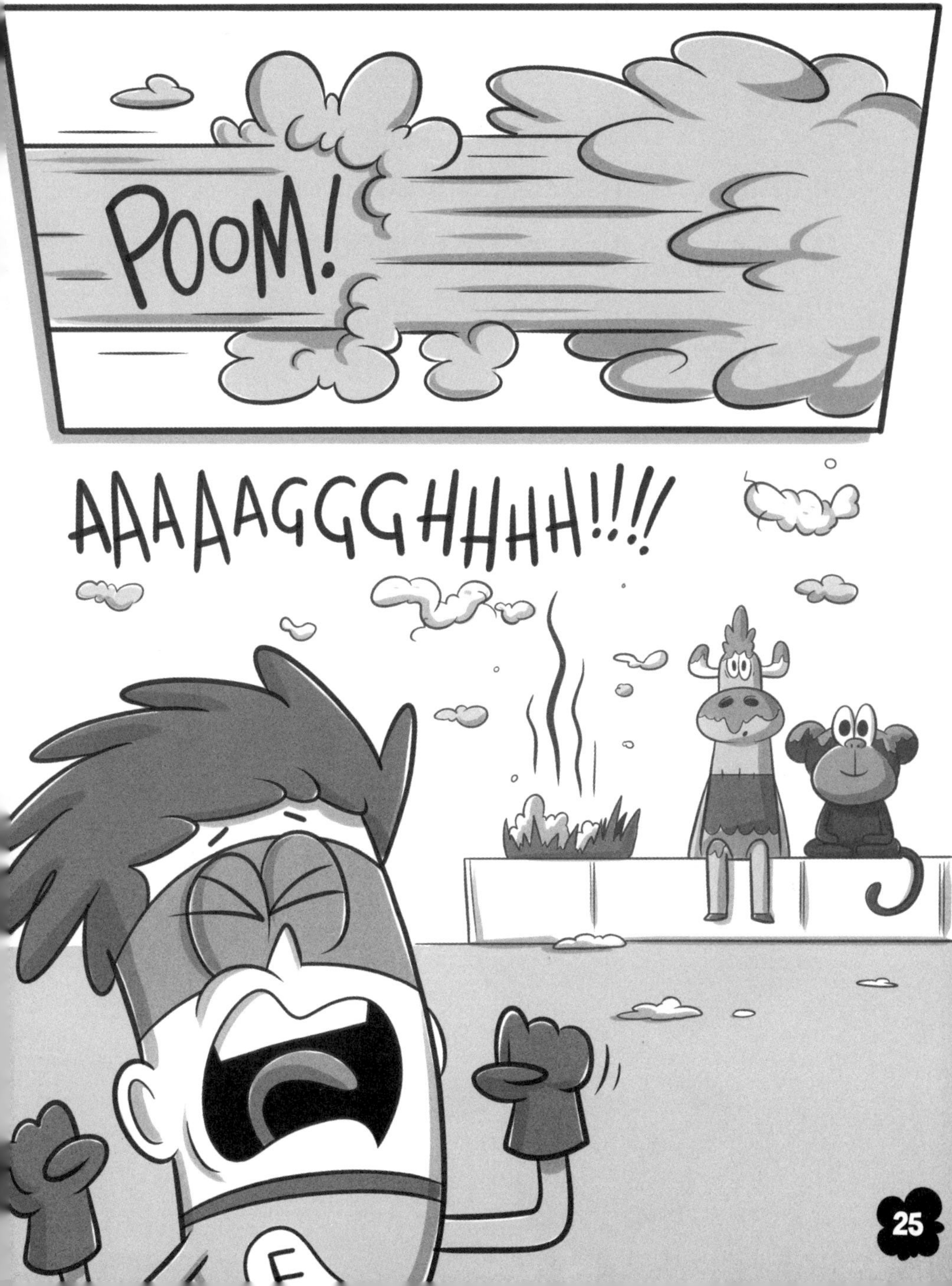
POOM!
AAAAAGGGHHHH!!!!

Grandma smiled and pulled out a device. 'Oh yeah, if you fart **too hard** you will blast everything to smithereens! **BEAN CLEAN** only occurs at one *very specific* fart frequency. You must hit exactly 4.3 on the **BUTT-CLENCHER SCALE.** Now try again.'

I tried again.

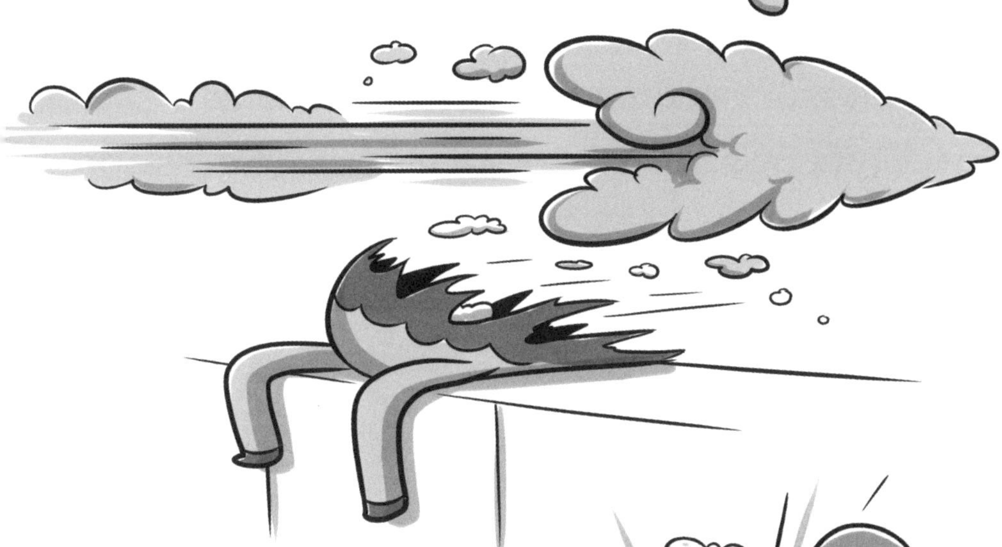
POOPHHH!

And again.

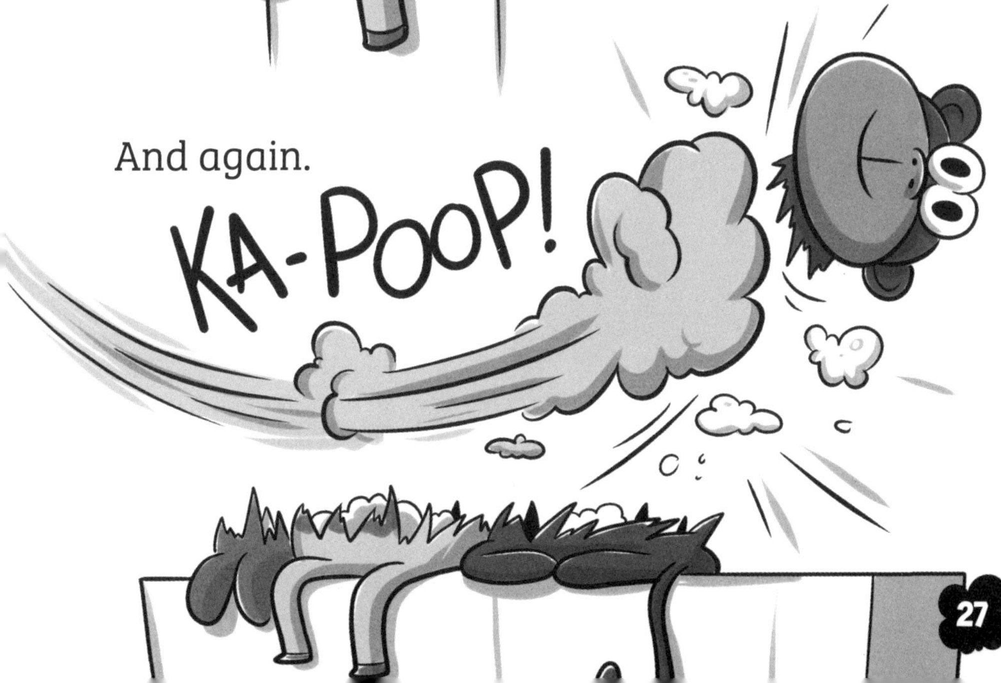
KA-POOP!

This was terrible!

'Right,' Grandma said. 'Before all your fluffy toys are destroyed, try this. To get a 4.3 on the **BUTT-CLENCHER**, you must squeeze your **right cheek** a little tighter, and your **left cheek** a little less. Your amazing **bott-bott-bazooka** will do the rest.'

Grandma rubbed mud on *Loopy Lou*.

I ate a baked bean, lined up, clenched, farted . . . and **blew** Loopy Lou **to smithereens!**

NOOOOOOOOO! LOOPY LOU!

That was a 7.4!

I tried again with Fifi.

It didn't end well for Fifi.

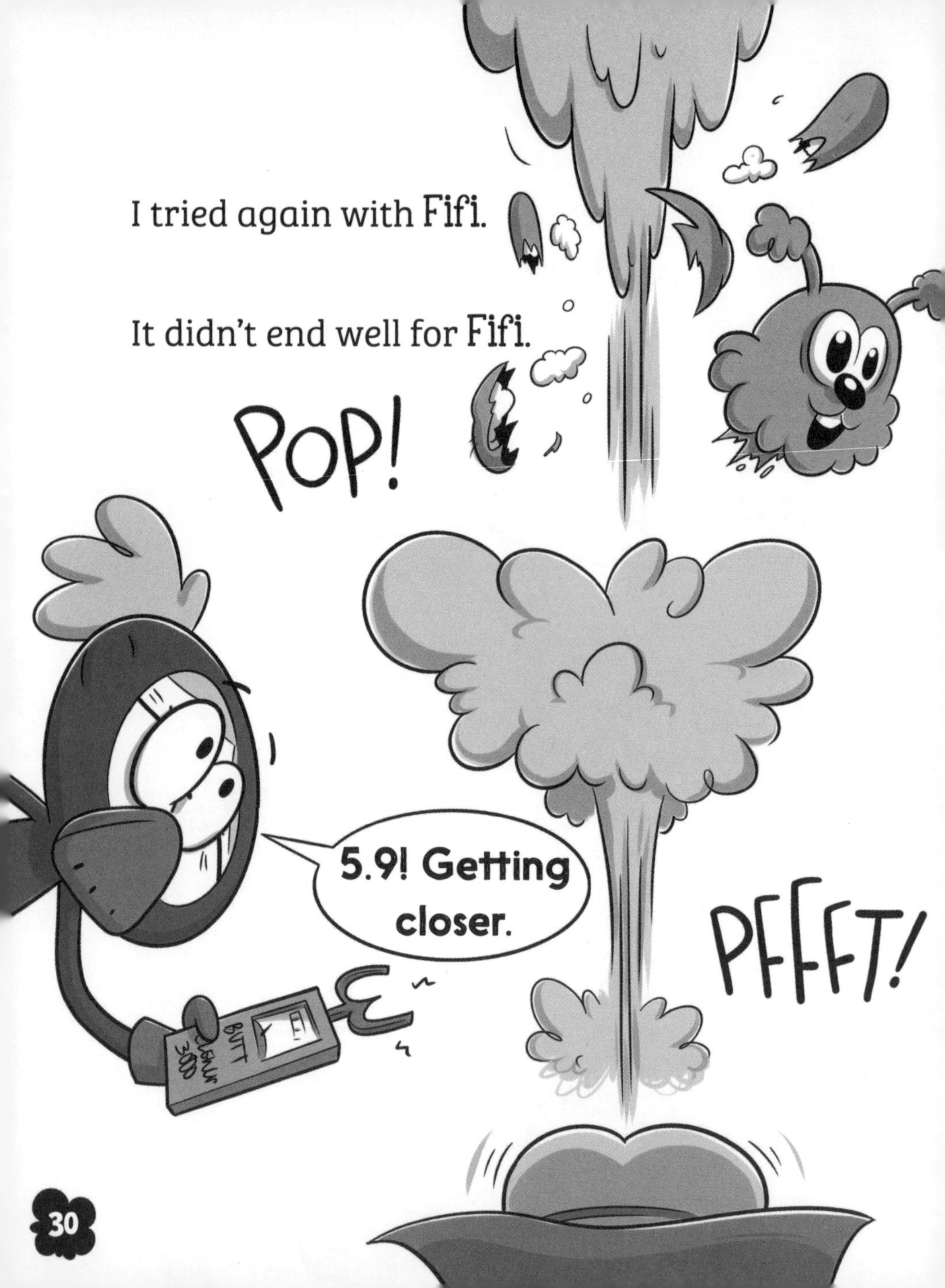
POP!
5.9! Getting closer.
PFFFT!

Or **Bright Eyes the Bunny.**

Whoops.
10.8!

Only **Sparkles the Unicorn** remained.

I closed my eyes and focused. I did a **lopsided clench.** I spoke to my bum. 'OK, bum, you can do this. I believe in your stinkiness!'

I held up a baked bean and I . . .

COULDN'T DO IT!

Not to **Sparkles!**

'I CAN'T RISK IT!' I screamed.

'I'll never blow you to smithereens, **Sparkles**,' I whispered.

If I couldn't fart things clean, I would have to defeat **SPEWTANK** by fighting dirty!

SQUIRT

A Very Happy Farter's Day

The next day I did a tour of Sparkletown with the **Tidy Town Committee.** It really was neat and tidy and clean and sparkly and shiny.

Even **Mr Hamilton's head** looked *extra* shiny. The Tidy Town judges were going to love us!

Next, at school, there was a special assembly with the Principal, **Mrs Manson.**

Even the news crew was there!

Today, the World's Tidiest Town Judging Committee is coming to Sparkletown. And to celebrate, I am giving away a prize for the tidiest classroom!

We all cheered. **Stewie and Alice,** my two best friends, had worked SO hard to help me keep our classroom really, really clean.

I high-fived Alice.

And I clapped Stewie on the back, making him spew into one of the **sick bags** he always carried around.

'I've been spewing more since the **BAKED BEANS FACTORY** explosion,' Stewie said. 'But I'm getting better at catching it.'

Alice scowled and picked rubbish out of her hair. She was really, really messy, **allllll the time.** She tried to be clean, like everyone else in Sparkletown, but it was really hard for her.

Mrs Manson continued. 'The prize for the **tidiest classroom** is a cruise on the brand-new **BAKED BEAN BOAT**. And the winner is . . .'

I held my breath and crossed my fingers. I really wanted to win.

CLASS 3F!

Class 3F? **That was us!** I whooped and cheered.

Stewie **spewed** into a sick bag.

Alice **spilt her drink.** I was so happy I didn't care . . . for five seconds, then I cleaned up after her.

But assembly wasn't over yet.
Mr Hamilton came in, dragging
a **mysterious object.**

'Sparkletown Primary School,' Mrs
Manson said. 'We are now the
proud owners of . . .

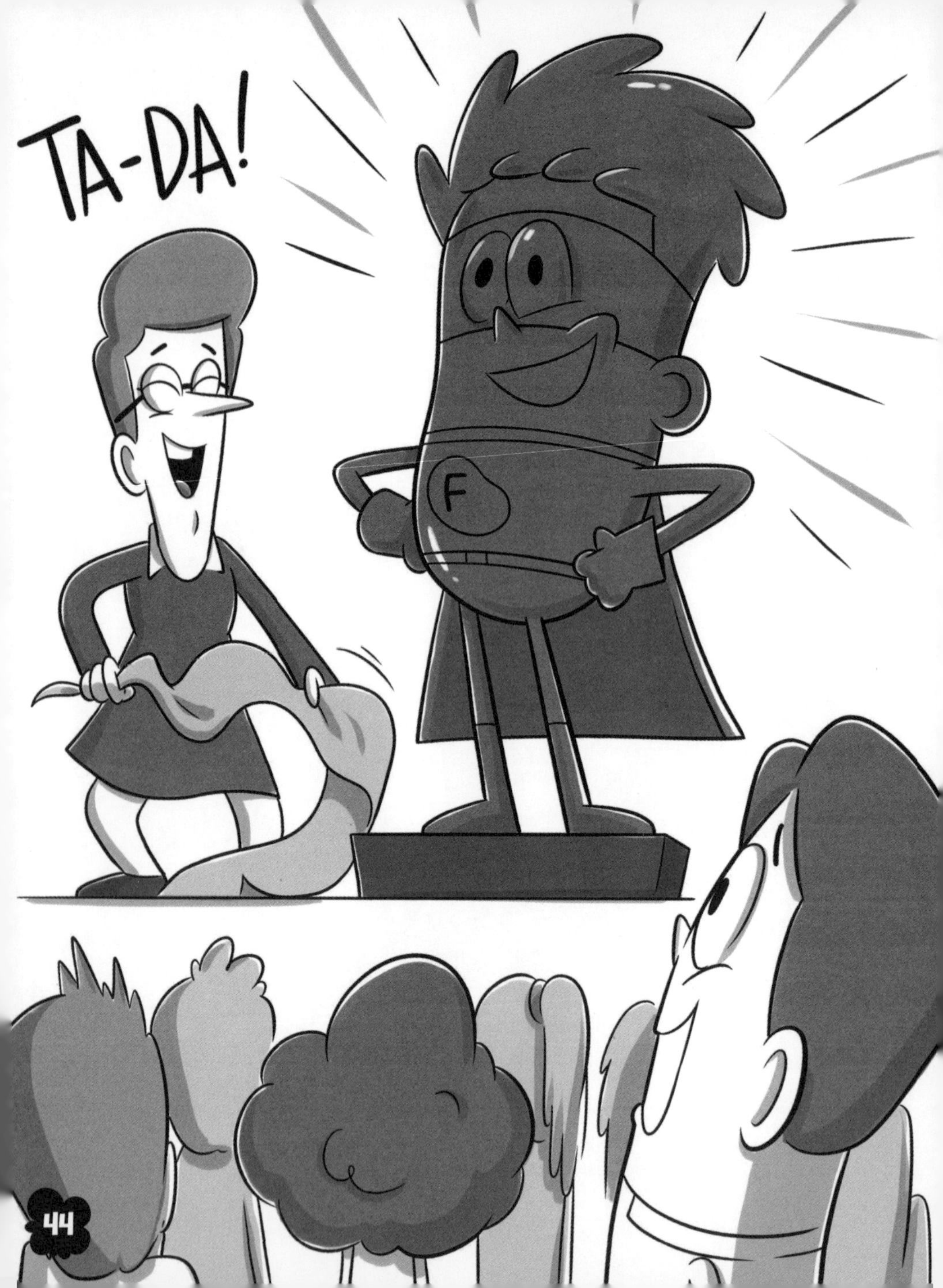
TA-DA!
F

A BRAND NEW STATUE!'

I couldn't believe my eyes. It was a Fartboy statue, and **it was AMAZING!**

Everyone cheered again and started chanting. **'FARTBOY! FARTBOY! FARTBOY!'**

A pigeon flew over and **pooped** on the statue. It reminded me of the day the **BAKED BEANS FACTORY** had exploded ... and **my parents went missing.** I cheered along with everyone else, but I wished my parents could have been there. That would have made it perfect.

NEWS FLASH!

We apologise for this interruption.

SPEWTANK has struck again, or should I say . . . **chucked** again! Hahahahaha, oh where do I come up with them?

In this latest, sick attack, it seems that **SPEWTANK** is trying to send a message to everyone in beautiful Sparkletown.

But the spew don't stick, **SPEWTANK**. The spew don't stick.

Come on, Fartboy, you *gaseous gargantuan,* put an end to this mess and win us that Tidy Town Title!

We now return you to your regular programming, *Meerkat Marriages.*

FARTS AHOY

The **BAKED BEAN BOAT** was waiting for us at the edge of the lake. As we boarded, I asked Alice and Stewie if they'd heard about **SPEWTANK'S** latest graffiti attack.

'Nope,' Stewie said. He leaned over the railing and vomited.

'Me neither,' said Alice, eating a banana and throwing her peel onto the pier.

I raced off and picked it up, then zoomed back onto the boat.

SWISH!

The Tidy Town judges were already in town, judging. They would meet the boat when we got back from our cruise. That's when they would inform me, head of the **Sparkletown Tidy Town Committee,** and everyone else, whether we were **the winners** or not.

Sparkletown had to be **perfect,** so I needed Alice to be clean and **SPEWTANK** to sleep in or go away on holiday somewhere!

Mrs Manson gathered us on the deck, and then we met the boat's Captain.

'**Hello, children,**' he said in a very deep voice. '**I am Captain Captain.**'

I gasped. 'Your surname is Captain?'

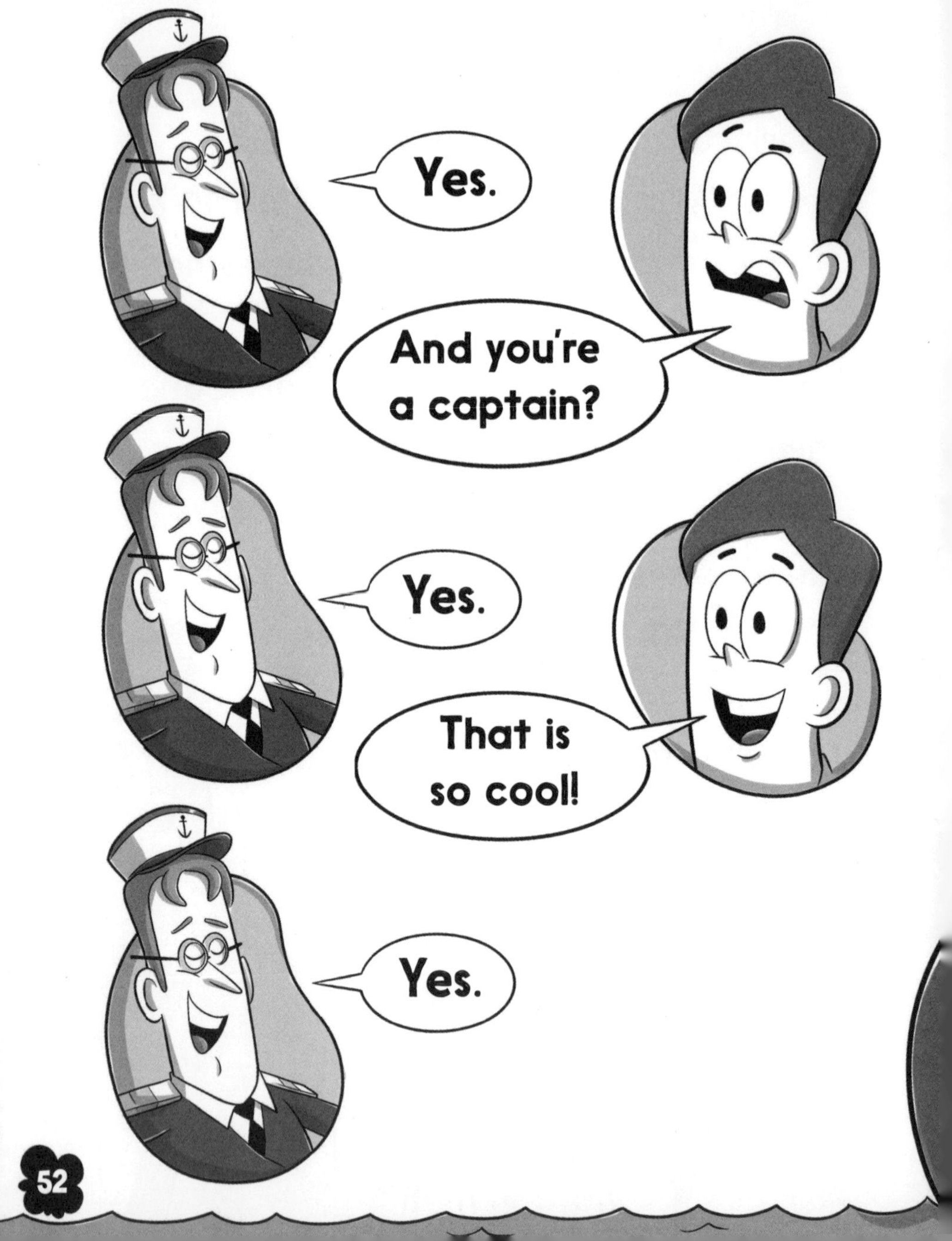
Yes.
And you're a captain?
Yes.
That is so cool!
Yes.

He started up the **BAKED BEAN BOAT**,
and it made a sound like a massive fart.

This was going to be . . .
hugely, **massively, titanically**
awesome!

Enter . . . The Tank!

The start of the cruise was amazing . . . and then **five things** happened!

1. STEWIE SPEWED FOR THE SIXTEENTH TIME SINCE THE CRUISE HAD STARTED.
2. ALICE TOOK STEWIE AWAY TO CLEAN UP.
3. WE SAW HEAPS OF FISH SWIMMING BESIDE THE BOAT.
4. SOMEBODY SCREAMED.
5. SP

We all ran to where the scream was, and then I screamed too! There was a message on the front of Captain Captain's captain's cabin . . . a message written in **chuck, chunder, spew!**

SPEWTANK was on the boat!

Three crew members came out with a hose to wash down the cabin, and that was when the **fifth thing** happened.

'TAKE THIS!!!'

It was a surprise attack! It was disgusting and horrible and terrible and awful! We got covered in vomit from head to toe.

I spun around, and then I was covered in vomit from face to face!

'Heh, heh, heh! Look at you now, *clean* class,' **SPEWTANK** said.

We looked. We wished we hadn't.

HEH

HEH HEH

HEH

HEH

'Why are you doing this?' I asked. As I spoke a piece of **carrot** dripped off my nose.

'Why?' asked **SPEWTANK.** '*Why?* Because of people like *YOU*, Martin Kennedy! All you talk about is the stupid **Tidy Town Competition.** All Sparkletown cares about is being **neat and clean and sparkly and shiny!** Well what about me? What about people who aren't clean? Where do we fit in here? What are we supposed to do?'

'BE CLEAN?'

'**NO!**' **SPEWTANK** screamed. 'Love us for who we are. **I will never be clean!** And when we get back to shore, I'm going to turn Sparkletown into **Spew City!**'

SPEWTANK hurled up a wall of vomit.

When the wall splashed down again . . . **SPEWTANK** was gone. We stood for a moment in shock, dripping in yucky-yucky-yuck-yuck.

Then Johnny Wallace cried out, **'WE NEED FARTBOY!'**

Everyone started chanting Fartboy's name. Sparkletown needed Fartboy, and it needed him now!

A SUSPECT iS SUSPECTED

While the **BAKED BEAN BOAT** crew hosed everyone down, I headed for the toilets to change into my costume. On the way, I bumped into my friends and quickly filled them in on **SPEWTANK'S** attack.

'I was waiting for Stewie outside the toilet,' Alice said. 'But I heard everyone screaming.'

'Where are *you* going, Martin?' asked Stewie. 'Aren't you going to help clean?'

Oh boy, that was a terrible excuse, but I'd panicked. I couldn't tell them I was Fartboy! I tried again. It got worse.

'ME NEED WEE REAL BAD!'

'Ooooooooooookay,' said Alice. As she spoke, a little bit of **vomit** fell onto the ground. Stewie must have got her.

I ran into a cubicle and changed into **Fartboy**.

Then I dashed outside, ate a bean and **farted onto the top of the cabin** to get a good view of the deck. I looked around and said the first thing that came into my head.

'**Ew.**' It really did look gross.

BRAAPP!!

Then Johnny Wallace spotted me and my whole class **roared their approval.**

I ate another baked bean and jumped off the cabin, puffing out a **stinky wind** to cushion my landing.

'Captain Captain,' I said, 'you hose the decks. I'll clean the cabin.'

FART SCHOOL had been a disaster. But, surely, this time I'd be able to control my clenches, and **BEAN CLEAN** successfully. I relaxed. **I clenched.** I let loose a blast of hot air.

POOM!

I blew the cabin to smithereens.

Whoops.

The cheering stopped. Everyone took a step backwards.

Captain Captain shook his head, turned the boat around and started heading for shore.

I felt **totally bummed.** Maybe I wasn't the hero they thought I was.

I couldn't rely on fart power to clean up **SPEWTANK'S** chunder. But maybe I could **stop the villain** *before* any more vomit was spewed.

Who was **SPEWTANK** really? One of my classmates?

Unfortunately, my mind kept coming back to **one person.**

A person who had been puking more since the **FACTORY EXPLOSION** that had given me my powers.

A person who wasn't on deck when **SPEWTANK** appeared.

A person who spewed **all the time.**

My best friend.

I was sure Stewie was SPEWTANK.

SO LONG, SPEWIE STEWIE!

The boat steamed towards the shore. A crowd had gathered on the pier, with the huge **Tidy Town Trophy** right in the middle.

The Tidy Town judges were there, waiting, and I still hadn't worked out how to stop **SPEWTANK,** but I kept my eye on Stewie.

POOT!

It *had* to be him. I didn't know if I could stop **SPEWTANK** in a battle, so I had to trick Stewie into hiding.

He leaned over the railing again, looking green. While Alice was off getting him **a sick bag,** I farted the dinghy into the water.

WOW! NICE!

OOOH! AH!

Then, chewing on half a baked bean, I aimed a medium, non-cleaning puff at Stewie.

There was no way he could change into his **SPEWTANK** costume out in the middle of the lake. I would come back for him later with Grandma, once the competition was over.

Everything was going to be OK!

THE KING OF THE HURL

Everything was **NOT** OK!

A sudden **power spew** knocked me to the ground and trapped Captain Captain and Class 3F in a **spew lagoon.**

SPLAT!

I farted myself clear. 'You!' I said. 'How?'

SPEWTANK laughed. 'I'll do whatever it takes to make sure Sparkletown LOSES the Tidy Town Competition!'

Soon, I will finally fit in!

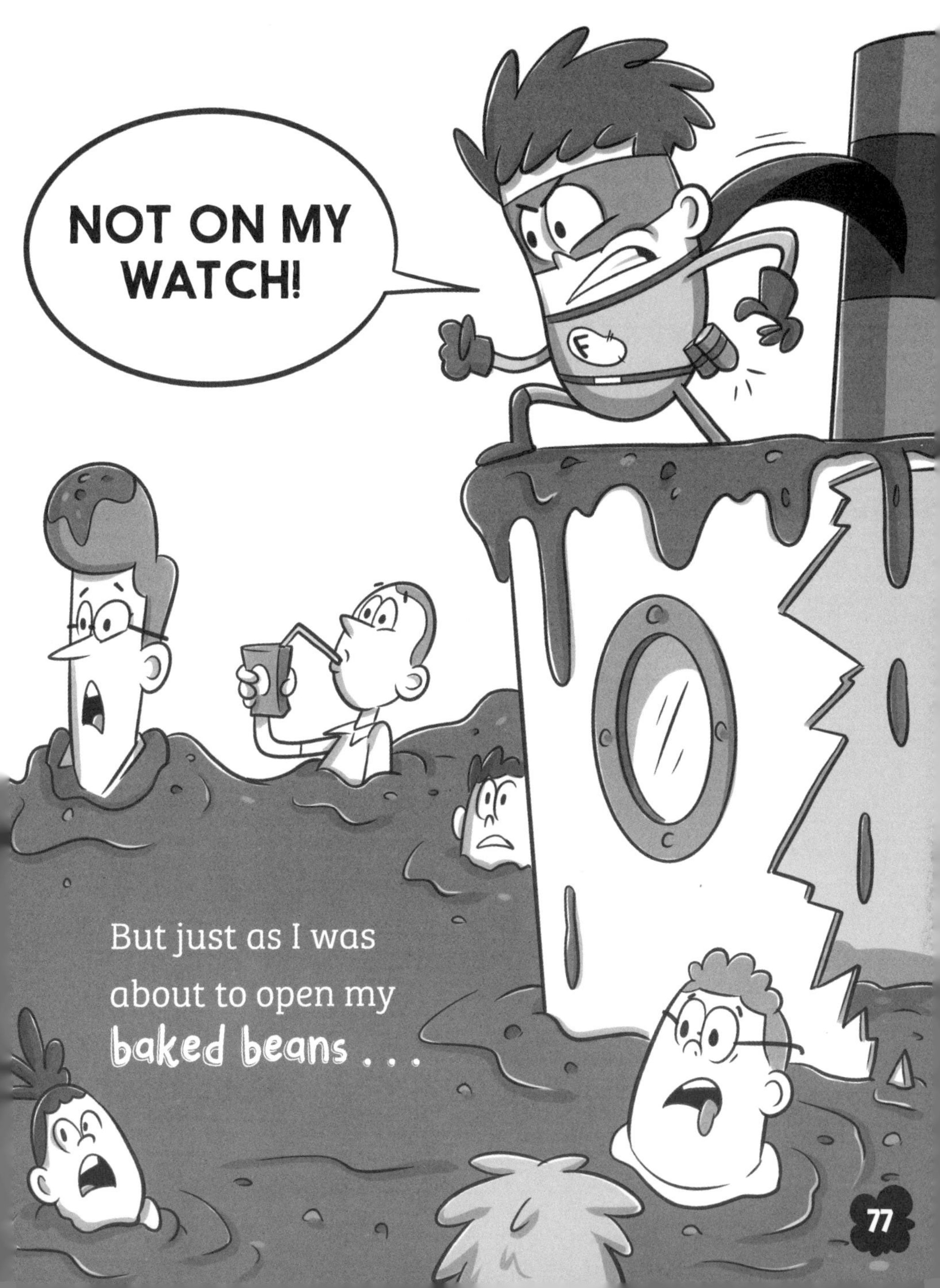
NOT ON MY WATCH!
But just as I was about to open my baked beans . . .

SPEWTANK knocked the can out of my hands with a well-aimed **vomit comet**. Powerless, I ran after it. But the can was flowing away down the **chunky river**.

SPEWTANK jumped to the front of the boat, and yelled, 'I'm about to hurl down on this town!'

I'M THE KING OF THE HURL!

I closed my eyes and dived, landing with a disgusting splash. I caught hold of my trusty baked beans can just before it dropped off the edge.

We were almost at the pier now. I saw Captain Captain clambering towards the boat's controls. I had to end this.

'**SPEWTANK**,' I yelled. 'It's time to take you and your half-eaten lunch down.

LET'S ROCK THIS FARTY!'

THE FiNaL ~~BuTTLe~~ BaTTLe

SPEWTANK spun around and attacked with a **mighty power puke.** It hit Captain Captain and knocked him back into the spew lagoon.

ARGH!

'No-one can stop me now!' Spewtank roared in triumph. 'This vomit-filled boat will destroy the pier and cover Sparkletown in messy, stinky spew!'

The villain's metal mouth **opened wide,** ready to hurl again.

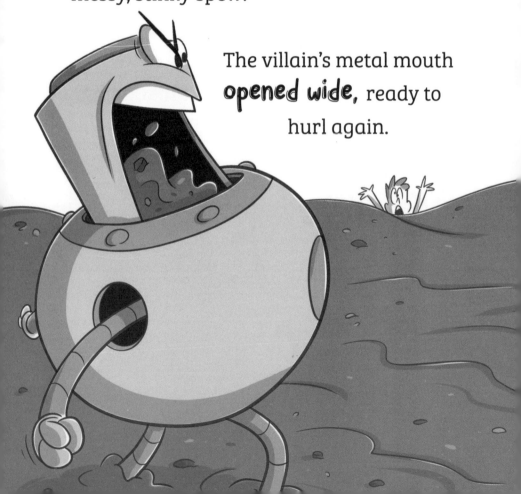

'But *I'll* stop you!' I said. I loaded up on baked beans, ready to **blow SPEWTANK into the water** like I had done with . . .

Wait. *Stewie?*

STEWIE WAS STANDING IN FRONT OF SPEWTANK.

STEWIE WASN'T **SPEWTANK!**

'**Don't worry, Fartboy!**' Stewie said. 'I can catch **SPEWTANK'S** spew in my sick bag!'

Before I could act, **Spewtank** sent a **torrent of vomit** right at Stewie.

EEEEEEEEEEEEEE

But the sick bag wasn't big enough, and poor Stewie was **VOMIT-BLASTED OFF THE BOAT!**

'The **cleanest best friend a boy could have** won't be able to help anyone now!' **SPEWTANK** gloated.

Hang on . . . *'Cleanest best friend?'* I had only said that in front of **two people.** One of them was up a tree, and the other was . . . *Alice?*

SPEWTANK leaned back and launched a **massive arc of yuckiness** over the entire pier, the people, and—oh no, *THE JUDGES!*

BLURRGH!

I **ran** across the deck, **slid** on my tummy, and **farted** high and long.

My **butt tornado** intercepted **SPEWTANK'S** spew arc and blasted it into smithereens. And that wasn't all! Next, the **smithereens of spew** exploded into **wonderful fireworks of chunder!**

Everyone on the pier **cheered**, thinking it was *real* fireworks.

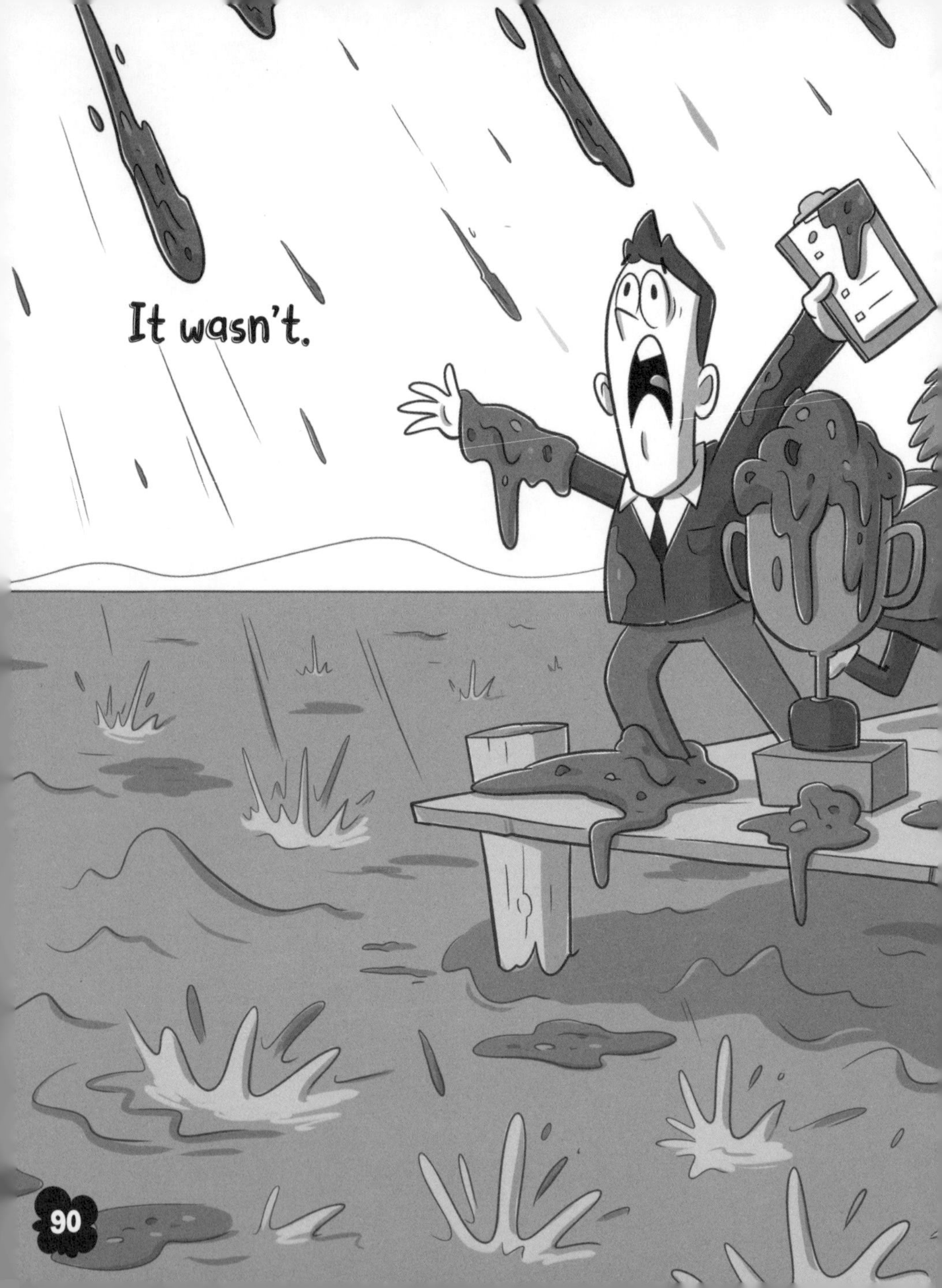
It wasn't.

The chunderworks came down and **splattered** all over the people, the pier and the lake. The usually crystal-clear water turned murky and thick.

Captain Captain finally got out of the **chunky lagoon** and stopped the boat just before it crashed into the pier.

But no-one was cheering.

And the judges looked **really angry.**

'This is **a disgrace,**' one of them said. 'I have **never** seen such a messy, disgusting town in my entire life!'

'HAHAHA!' SPEWTANK laughed. 'You've lost! **Sparkletown** has finally lost!'

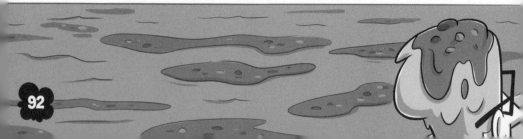

'Oh really?' a voice from the pier said. I looked over. **It was Grandma!**

'Really!' said Spewtank. 'That judge said so!'

'What you don't know, **SPEWTANK,** is that Fartboy has the power to clean like the **stinkiest reverse vacuum cleaner** in the world.'

GULP!

ISN'T THAT RIGHT, FARTBOY?

All my classmates, even the one stuck high up a tree, were staring at me in hope.

The judges were staring at me in grumpiness.

SPEWTANK was staring at me in anger.

And Grandma was staring at me with belief.

This was it. The fate of the entire town rested with me. Not only that, I was either about to do a **4.3 clencher** and clean up the town, save the day, possibly win the **World's Tidiest Town** for the eighteenth year straight and also ruin **SPEWTANK'S** plans.

Or I would **blast everyone to smithereens.**

So yeah.
There was that.

THUNDERSTRUCK

I had never been more nervous. I was **SHAKING AT THE KNEES**.

'Come on then, Fluff Butt,' **SPEWTANK** said, standing between me and the pier. 'Clean up **my lovely mess** . . . if you can.'

I closed my eyes. I clenched. It felt right. But then I remembered my **fluffy toys** being **blasted** to bits!

I couldn't do it.

And then I heard it. It started with a **little old lady's voice.** 'Fartboy, Fartboy, Fartboy!'

Then Mrs Manson and **my classmates** joined in. 'Fartboy, Fartboy, Fartboy!'

Then **everyone on the pier** joined in. 'FARTBOY! FARTBOY! FARTBOY!'

Even **Captain Captain** joined in.
FARTBOY! FARTBOY! FARTBOY!

I clenched **a little to the right.** I
released **my left butt cheek** a little.

I felt it! **I felt the 4.3 Butt-Clencher!**

I shoved **twenty-seven baked beans** in my mouth, and I let fly.

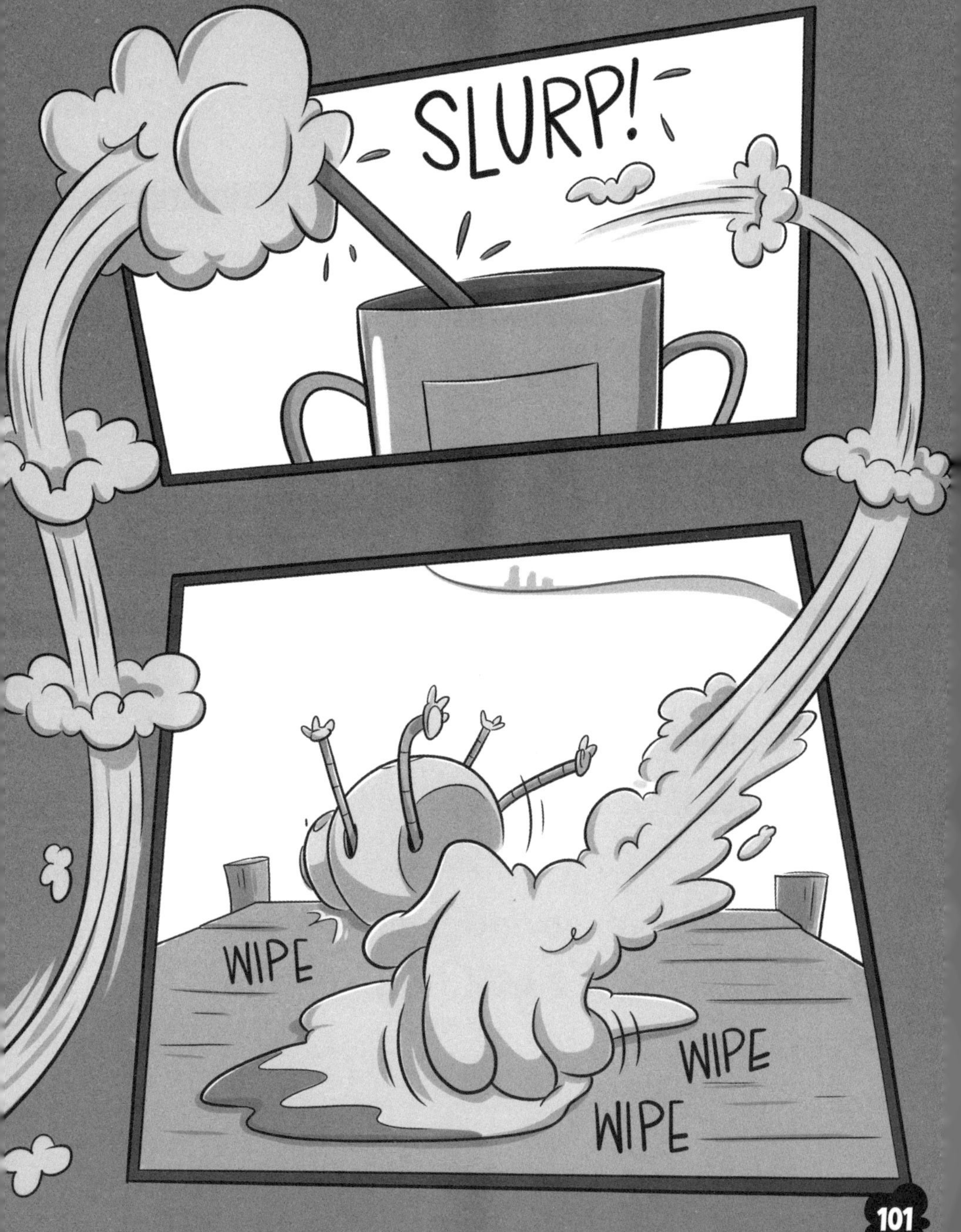
SLURP!
WIPE
WIPE
WIPE

When the **BEAN CLEAN** finally finished, I couldn't believe it. Sparkletown and the **BAKED BEAN BOAT** and all the people were cleaner than ever!

While everyone was passed out from the smelly fart's assault on their nostrils, I ran over to **SPEWTANK** and woke her up.

She looked at me, embarrassed and defeated.

'Alice,' I said, 'go and change. No-one else knows it's you. Only me. And I won't tell.'

'But how do *you* know?' she asked. 'Who are you?'

'I'm your best friend!' I said.

'What? No! **Stewie's up a tree.** Your *other* best friend.'

Alice relaxed. 'I'm so sorry, Martin,' she said. 'I got spew powers after I was frozen in baked-bean earwax. And I felt like I didn't belong here. I love this town, but **it doesn't love me.**'

I didn't want to admit it, but **she was right.** Everything in Sparkletown was about being clean.

If you were someone **naturally messy,** like Alice, you didn't fit in. But maybe there was something we could do.

'Everyone's about to wake up,' I said. 'But I have an idea. Become a superhero, Alice. With me. We'll be a team. **The grossest superhero team ever.** You may be messy, but you belong in this town. Everyone here loves cleaning. And without messy people like you, we'd have no-one to clean up after.'

Alice thought about it, and then she smiled a smile only a **best friend** could smile. She gave me a **messy, vomity hug** and then ran off to change.

I did too. I had to be **Martin Kennedy** again when the judges woke up. I could only hope that they had forgiven the **vomit fireworks.**

TIDYING EVERYTHING UP

Everyone stood on the pier, waiting . . .

Everyone except for **Captain Captain.**
He was still on board the brand-new
BAKED BEAN BOAT which didn't look
brand new anymore . . .

The judges were in a huddle, making their **final decision.**

The huddle broke up.

They walked over and stood in front of the crowd and the **World's Tidiest Town trophy.**

'Ladies and Gentlemen,' said the head judge (this meant he was the main judge, not that he judged heads). 'Those vomit fireworks were the **most disgusting thing** in the history of the world, and placed you last in the **World's Tidiest Town Competition.**'

'**Ohhhhhhhh,**' sighed everyone. Alice hung her head.

'However, the boat didn't crash into the pier and destroy it!'

'YAAAAAAAY!'

the crowd cheered.

'But the vomit was still disgusting.'

'Ohhhhhhhh.'

'And the kid in the funny suit did the **biggest pop-off** since the cavemen, which then placed you **lower than last.'**

'Ohhhhhhhhh.'

Was lower than last even possible?

'But then we had a nap.'

'YAAAAAAAAY!'

'And when we woke
up, there was still
six seconds of judging
time left.'

'YAAAAAAAAY?'

'But it was still stinky.'

'**Ohhhhhhhhh.**'

'But we have never, ever, ever in our lives . . .' He paused.

We all held our breath . . .

And then the head judge said the sweetest words possible.

'... **EVER** seen a town more **neat and tidy and clean and sparkly and shiny** than this one. **Congratulations, Sparkletown, you are the World's Tidiest Town for the eighteenth year straight!'**

I couldn't believe it! This was **THE GREATEST MOMENT OF MY LIFE!!!!**

Everyone on the pier jumped around cheering and hugging and high-fiving.

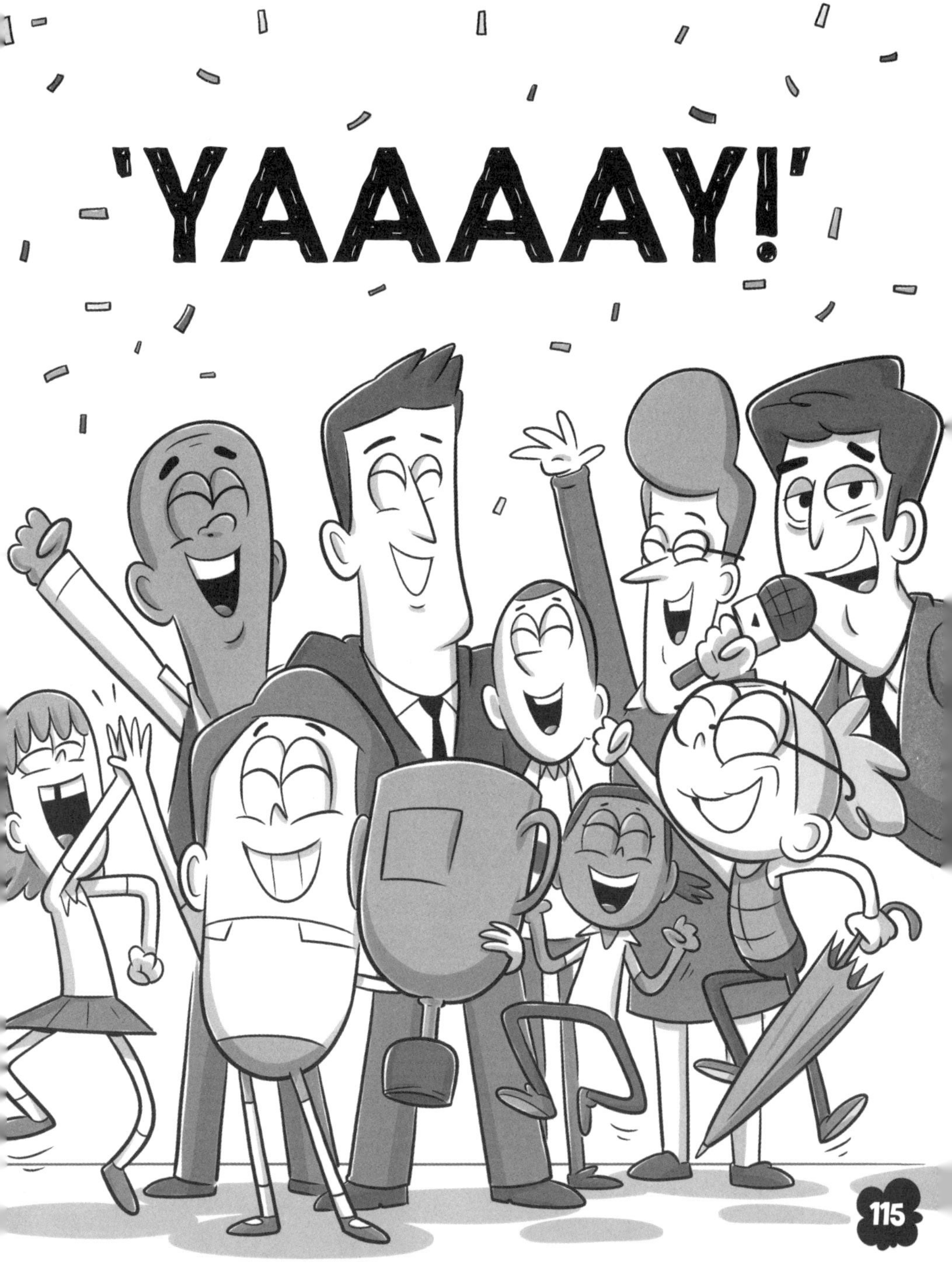
'YAAAAY!'

Everyone jumped around so much that we all fell into the water! Luckily, it wasn't very deep, but everyone held their breath, wondering how the judges would react.

We needn't have worried. The head judge flicked water at Mr Hamilton and cried,

WATER FIGHT!

CRYSTAL CLEAR

Everyone cheered again.

I smiled at Alice. She **flicked water** at me. I laughed and **flicked some back.** We were going to make a great team.

NEWS FLASH!

WE APOLOGISE FOR THS INTERRUPTION.

Boy breaks wind, and Sparkletown breaks record! Once again, **Fartboy has saved Sparkletown.**

And twice again, he did it using his **powerful bott bott.**

He's really full of hot air, that boy.

TRIBUTE
BEANS
BLOW IN!

Sparkletown has won the **World's Tidiest Town** for the eighteenth year straight, and in an announcement by Mayor McClure, the prize money will be used to rebuild and reopen the **BAKED BEANS FACTORY!**

All previous employees will get their old jobs back, and soon Sparkletown will be **making the world fart again!**

In other news, I had toast for breakfast. In other, other news, **SPEWTANK** has issued an apology. It was very long and detailed.

Sorry.

Riiiiiiight. Well, good enough for me! We now return you to your regular programming, *Californian Crazy Cats!*

PLEEEEEEEEEEASE!!!

I turned to Grandma. 'Mum and Dad are still missing,' I said. 'So *they* won't get their old jobs back.'

Grandma hugged me close. 'I know, Martin. But guess what? In all the excitement today, I clean forgot!

THERE'S A CLUE!'

I jumped out of my seat. 'Really? What is it, Grandma? Tell me! I'll go find them now!'

Grandma looked at me. She was either trying to work out whether to tell me, or she was **holding in a fart.** I knew she would never hold one in, so it had to be the other thing.

'Grandma, *pleeeeeeeease*. I have to know.'

'OK, Martin,' Grandma said. 'Here it is. Someone sent **these** to the police. Are you ready?'

'Of course I am, Grandma! Don't hold it in, **show me!**'

She showed me. I couldn't believe it! It was my parents. They were alive!

GRANDMA!
GRANDMA, IT'S THEM!

'Yes,' Grandma said. 'But now you have to sleep. It's been a huge day. **Tomorrow, we follow the clues.** I just hope there won't be some other *gross villain* who gets in our way.'

Grandma was right. I was exhausted. As I headed to bed, she called out. **'Oh, and Martin?'**

'Yes, Grandma?'

'Your parents would be **so proud of you.'**

I nodded, trying not to cry. Then I brushed my teeth and **went to sleep.**

As I drifted off, I imagined all the people on the pier **chanting for Fartboy.**

FARTBOY! FARTBOY!

FARTBOY! FARTBOY!

FARTBOY!

Only this time, when I saw it, it was slightly different. This time, **my parents were there too,** and they were chanting loudest of all.